This book
belongs to

_____

_____

David&Charles
Children's Books

To Toby with love
R.S.

For my baby brother
A.R.

First published in Great Britain in 1998
by Levinson Children's Books.
Published in this edition in 1999 by
David & Charles Children's Books,
Winchester House, 259-269 Old Marylebone Road,
London, NW1 5XJ

10 9 8 7 6 5 4 3 2 1

Text copyright © Ragnhild Scamell 1998
Illustrations copyright © Adrian Reynolds 1998

The right of Ragnhild Scamell and Adrian Reynolds
to be identified as the author and illustrator of this work has been asserted by
them in accordance with the Copyright, Designs and Patents Act 1988.

A CIP catalogue record for this title is available from the British Library.

Hardback ISBN 1 86233 026 3
Paperback ISBN 1 86233 067 0

Printed and bound in Italy

TOBY'S DOLL'S HOUSE

Written by **Ragnhild Scamell**
Illustrated by **Adrian Reynolds**

David&Charles
Children's Books

Toby wanted a doll's house for his birthday.
A beautiful doll's house with
an upstairs and a downstairs
and a front that opened up.

"He doesn't mean a doll's house," said Grandad.
"He means a fort. I always wanted a fort,
when I was a boy."

"No, no," said Auntie. "He means a farmyard.
A really large farmyard, with horses and cows,
and pigs and sheep."

"Of course he doesn't," said Dad.
"What Toby wants is a multi-storey
car-park full of toy cars."

But Toby knew exactly what he wanted.

He had already made some furniture from empty
matchboxes and bits of cardboard and Plasticine.
He had even cut out some people from a magazine.

They were all ready to move in.

"All I want is a doll's house," he said.
"A beautiful doll's house with an upstairs,
and a downstairs, and a front that opens up."

But nobody heard Toby.

Then Toby's special day arrived.

"Happy Birthday!" said Grandad
and handed Toby a large green parcel.

Inside the green wrapping paper was a large cardboard box
with a magnificent fort, which Grandad had made himself.

The fort had a drawbridge, and turrets, and a portcullis,
and it came with a plastic bag full of soldiers.

Toby lifted it all out and put
the cardboard box to one side.

"Thank you, Grandad," Toby said,
and he gave his grandad a hug.

"Happy Birthday, Toby!" said Auntie
and handed Toby a big red parcel.

Inside the red wrapping paper was a big box with a
wonderful farmyard. It had a pigsty, and a cowshed,
and a plastic bag full of farm animals.

Toby lifted it all out and put
the cardboard box to one side.

"Thank you, Auntie,"
he said and he gave
his auntie a hug.

"Happy Birthday, Toby!" said Dad
and he handed Toby a huge parcel.

Inside the blue wrapping paper was an enormous cardboard box with a multi-storey car-park. It had lanes going up and lanes going down. There were parking spaces on three floors and a plastic bag full of toy cars.

Toby lifted it all out on the floor and put the huge box on top of the two smaller cardboard boxes.

"Thank you, Dad," he said, and gave his dad a hug.

And as Grandad set out the fort
and Auntie set out the farmyard
and Dad set out the
multi-storey car-park...

Toby drew some windows on the
sides of his doll's house and a door.

Then he put the doll's house on the green
wrapping paper. It looked just like grass.

He used the red wrapping paper to make a roof.

Toby drew some windows on the
sides of his doll's house and a door.

Then he put the doll's house on the green
wrapping paper. It looked just like grass.

He used the red wrapping paper to make a roof.

And when he opened his eyes again,
he could hardly believe what he saw.
There it was, a beautiful doll's house...

... with an upstairs,

and a downstairs,

and a front that opened up.

...Toby blew out the candles on his birthday cake.
He closed his eyes and made a wish.

Toby wished that he had a doll's house.

And he cut up the blue wrapping paper and carpeted all
the rooms in his doll's house. Then he put the furniture in.
Some upstairs and some downstairs.

Finally, the people were ready to move in.
Toby gave them each a small piece of
birthday cake. Everyone was happy.

The cut-out dolls in their new house.
Grandad with his fort.
Auntie with her farmyard.
And Dad with his multi-storey car-park.

But happiest of them all was Toby.

And while the soldiers marched around
in their fort, and the farm animals went "Neigh!",
"Moo!", "Oink!" and "Baa!" in their yard,
and the cars moved noisily up and down their lanes,
the cut-out people finished eating their cake downstairs.

When they had finished, Toby put them to bed upstairs. And then he closed the front of the doll's house to give them a bit of peace and quiet.

Tomorrow, he would make some flowers for their garden.

Other David & Charles Picture Books
for you to read:

Eggday
JOYCE DUNBAR • JANE CABRERA
hardback: 1 86233 100 6

Waiting For Baby
HARRIET ZIEFERT • EMILY BOLAM
hardback: 1 86233 125 1

Another Fine Mess
TONY BONNING • SALLY HOBSON
hardback: 1 86233 094 8
paperback: 1 86233 145 6

Hugo and the Bully Frogs
FRANCESCA SIMON • CAROLINE JAYNE CHURCH
hardback: 1 86233 093 X

Animal ABC
DAVID WOJTOWYCZ
hardback: 1 86233 107 3

David&Charles
Children's Books